Asymmetry

by Rick Robinson

A SAMUEL FRENCH ACTING EDITION

SAMUEL FRENCH

FOUNDED 1830

NEW YORK HOLLYWOOD LONDON TORONTO

SAMUELFRENCH.COM

ISBN 978-0-573-65068-0   Printed in U.S.A.   #3827

MUSIC USE NOTE

Licensees are solely responsible for obtaining formal written permission from copyright owners to use copyrighted music in the performance of this play and are strongly cautioned to do so. If no such permission is obtained by the licensee, then the licensee must use only original music that the licensee owns and controls. Licensees are solely responsible and liable for all music clearances and shall indemnify the copyright owners of the play and their licensing agent, Samuel French, Inc., against any costs, expenses, losses and liabilities arising from the use of music by licensees.

**IMPORTANT BILLING AND CREDIT
REQUIREMENTS**

All producers of *ASYMMETRY must* give credit to the Author of the Play in all programs distributed in connection with performances of the Play, and in all instances in which the title of the Play appears for the purposes of advertising, publicizing or otherwise exploiting the Play and/or a production. The name of the Author *must* appear on a separate line on which no other name appears, immediately following the title and *must* appear in size of type not less than fifty percent of the size of the title type.

ASYMMETRY premiered in Los Angeles on October 8, 2005 as part of the 2005 Edge of the World Festival produced by Lucid By Proxy; Shannon Nelson, David Nett, Valerie Rachelle, Patty Ramsey, Rick Robinson, Jeanette Scherrer & James Paul Xavier, producers. The Light Designer was David Nett. The Costume Designer was Shannon Nelson. The Props and Set Dressing was by James Paul Xavier. The production was under the direction of Rick Robinson with the following cast:

SANDY	Melody Doyle
MIGUEL	Alex Fernandez
JULIUS	Alan Loayza
PRISCILLA	Shannon Nelson
CODY	David Nett
MAGGIE	Keaton Talmadge

ASYMMETRY was subsequently produced by Lucid by Proxy at the Paul E. Richards Theater Place in Los Angeles on October 20,2006. The Light Designers were Rick Robinson & Patty Ramsey. The Costume Designer was Shannon Nelson. The Props and Set Dressing was by James Paul Xavier. The production was under the direction of Rick Robinson and Patty Ramsey with the following cast:

SANDY	Melody Doyle
MIGUEL	Alex Fernandez
JULIUS	Alan Loayza
PRISCILLA	Shannon Nelson
CODY	David Nett
MAGGIE	Kyra Zagorsky

CHARACTERS

JULIUS

PRISCILLA

SANDY

MIGUEL

CODY

MAGGIE

*(The living room of a one bedroom apartment in San Jose,
present day. There are three doors that lead into and out of
the space: The bedroom, bathroom and a door to the outside world. A couch, sofa chair and coffee table sit on one
side of the stage, a small bar with two stools on the other.*
*There's a knock at the front door. JULIUS, 22, pokes his head
out the bedroom door dressed in a button up shirt so new it
still has its packaging creases.)*

JULIUS. *(O.S.)* Come in!

*(After briefly scurrying to straighten things up, JULIUS takes a
deep breath and answers the door. PRISCILLA, 23, stands
at the threshold, looking like she's ready to bolt at the first
sign of trouble. She hides the left side of her face behind a
curtain of hair.)*

JULIUS. *(Cont.)* Hi! Hey. Welcome.
PRISCILLA. Hi.
JULIUS. Are you going to come in?
PRISCILLA. Thank you.
JULIUS. Your hair looks really different from your photo.
PRISCILLA. Oh.
JULIUS. No, not in a bad way.
PRISCILLA. I'm sorry, maybe I should go...

ASYMMETRY

JULIUS. No, no, no, no, no. No. Let me take your bag. You really can stay, Priscilla.

(Reluctantly, she hands over her jungle-themed luggage.)

JULIUS. *(Cont.)* Hey, this is nice. You just getting back from a safari?

PRISCILLA. Where are you going?

JULIUS. What?

PRISCILLA. I thought I was staying on the couch...

JULIUS. Right. Oh, right. My fault. How about... *(Placing the bag at the foot of the couch.)* ... here.

PRISCILLA. Thank you.

(Pause.)

JULIUS. So did you eat on the plane or...?

PRISCILLA. Peanuts.

JULIUS. Well, you know, I hope those will last ya. I already ate.

PRISCILLA. I'm fine.

JULIUS. No, I'm just kidding. I have reservations. Traatorr-riia something or other. I was totally kidding. It's Italian. I-tal-i-a-no, right? Oh, I have to cook something for you. You know, not tonight, but tomorrow.

PRISCILLA. Julius.

JULIUS. Chicken Cacciatore! C'mon. And pasta...? You're not on a low carb thing or anything?

PRISCILLA. Julius?

JULIUS. Yes?

PRISCILLA. I have something to show you.

JULIUS. Is it a present?

ASYMMETRY

(She crosses to the couch and sits, waiting for him to do the same.)

PRISCILLA. No.

JULIUS. I didn't get you anything.

PRISCILLA. Please. Can you sit?

JULIUS. The reservations are for like... okay. *(He sits.)* Okay, shoot. Wait, what's the matter. Priscilla?

PRISCILLA. I'm sorry. *(Collecting herself.)* Do you remember how you said last month in the chat room... you said you could be with me no matter what I looked like.

JULIUS. Listen, you're beautiful. I'm sorry I didn't say it when you first came in, but...

PRISCILLA. *(Stopping him.)* No. She pulls back the curtain of hair covering the left side of her face to reveal a long scar that runs from her eyebrow to her jaw.

(JULIUS starts to say something and stops. His moment to ease her fears passes.)

PRISCILLA. I thought if anybody could... I don't know. Are you going to say something?

JULIUS. Wow.

PRISCILLA. 'Wow'?

JULIUS. What? It's not a big deal.

PRISCILLA. Julius...

JULIUS. I don't care that your face is all messed up.

PRISCILLA. What?

JULIUS. *(On the move.)* You ready to go? It's not a big deal. What do you want me to say?

PRISCILLA. Not *that*.

ASYMMETRY

JULIUS. I'm adjusting, okay? How long have we known each other?

PRISCILLA. Officially?

JULIUS. No, online. From the poker group. It just seems like...

PRISCILLA. Yes?

JULIUS. It just seems like... you know... maybe you could have mentioned it.

PRISCILLA. When, Julius, in between-

JULIUS. Just slipped it in...

PRISCILLA. *(Overlapping.)* -raise you fifty-

JULIUS. ...somewhere, you know-

PRISCILLA. *(Overlapping.)* And I have two pair?

JULIUS. Like you know, I was bit by a dog, or hey, oops cut myself, or hey, Julius, that picture that I sent you, the one in the heart? Well, my hair was covering my shark bite. What? I said it's not a big deal.

PRISCILLA. It is a big deal.

JULIUS. It just seems, I don't know... It just seems a little dishonest.

PRISCILLA. I was in an accident, okay?

(She collapses on the couch in tears. JULIUS, utterly out of his element, interprets this as a moment he needs to console her.)

JULIUS. I'm sorry. That wasn't fair.

PRISCILLA. No.

JULIUS. I'm sorry.

PRISCILLA. I'm not a beauty queen.

JULIUS. What, you think I'm some kind of beauty... king?

PRISCILLA. Julius.

ASYMMETRY

JULIUS. I'm not. I have things, too. *(Pointing to his chin.)* Look. See this scar?

PRISCILLA. That's not the same thing.

JULIUS. No, wait. I got it when I fell off a merry-go-round. How's that for 'tough guy'? You know? It wasn't even one of the one's that went up and down. My sister laughed until she saw the blood.

PRISCILLA. *(Softening.)* Not the same thing.

JULIUS. I have flaws. Plenty. You want, you say something you don't like about me.

PRISCILLA. No.

JULIUS. Anything at all.

PRISCILLA. That's okay.

JULIUS. Small forehead. Weak chin. Dorky glasses. You know, hair all... you know...

PRISCILLA. Sweet though.

JULIUS. I have a little head. Sheldon Weidon said I looked like had one of those shrunken head things.

PRISCILLA. You do have kind of little head.

JULIUS. You see? Evens. You know, now that I look at you...

(As JULIUS reaches over to wipe the tears from her eyes PRISCILLA grabs his hand aggressively. Instinctively.)

JULIUS. *(Retreating.)* Whoah.

PRISCILLA. *(Standing.)* Please.

JULIUS. I'm sorry, I...

PRISCILLA. No, I didn't mean to-

JULIUS. *(Overlapping.)* I'm sorry... you have a line-

PRISCILLA. I don't like to be touched. You just came at me.

ASYMMETRY

JULIUS. *(Overlapping.)* -and I crossed it.
PRISCILLA. I'm not ready yet, okay?
JULIUS. Totally fine.
PRISCILLA. We'll save the physical stuff...?
JULIUS. Of course. Like I said.

(Pause.)

JULIUS. So...
PRISCILLA. Is this place fancy?
JULIUS. You know. Not really. You look fine. There's only like a small dress code or something. Why, did you bring something else?
PRISCILLA. Yes.
JULIUS. You look good.
PRISCILLA. Julius.
JULIUS. You look really good. You know... for a place maybe a little more casual.
PRISCILLA. Julius.
JULIUS. You ready?
PRISCILLA. I need to use your shower.
JULIUS. Oh. Okay. We might be late. Okay, let me, umm... Ssssssure.

(He bolts to the bathroom to check to make sure it's clean enough for his guest.)

PRISCILLA. That's not weird, is it?
JULIUS. *(Re-emerging.)* Nothing's weird, Priscilla. Weird is all perspective. Can I call you Priscilla?
PRISCILLA. What else would you call me?
JULIUS. I don't know. Miss Strickland?

ASYMMETRY

PRISCILLA. Yes.
JULIUS. Because I can, you know.
PRISCILLA. I would like that.
JULIUS. Oh. Ok. *(Ceremonial.)* Miss Strickland.

(He opens the door to the bathroom for her.)

JULIUS. Your shower, Miss Strickland.
PRISCILLA. Thank you, sir.
JULIUS. My lady. I shall await you four score. *(Pause.)*
Hey Priscilla?
PRISCILLA. Yeah?
JULIUS. I'm sorry. Totally new me, from this point on.
PRISCILLA. Me too.
JULIUS. Okay.
PRISCILLA Okay.
JULIUS. *(Lingering.)* See you after your shower.
PRISCILLA. Okay.

*(She closes the door. JULIUS paces back and forth across his
living room, rehearsing under his breath.*
*MIGUEL, 44, enters from the bedroom. He wears clothes sized
to fit his more formidable former self and a skull-cap to
hide his baldness.*
*JULIUS stops his pacing short suddenly, remembering that he
didn't give PRISCILLA a towel. He exits past MIGUEL into
the bedroom, neither one of them aware of the other's pres-
ence.*
*MIGUEL looks at himself in the mirror, running his hand over
his gaunt cheek. A knock summons him to the front door.
He stops just shy of it, collects himself, then opens the door
to his past.)*

ASYMMETRY

SANDY. Hi.

MIGUEL. *(Fondly.)* Sandy Brown.

SANDY. Miguel.

MIGUEL. Come in, come in.

SANDY. How are you?

(She hugs him.)

SANDY. You look good.

MIGUEL. Thank you.

SANDY. *(Taking in the room.)* It's nice.

MIGUEL. *(Laughing.)* That's two lies in like what... five seconds?

SANDY. I'm sorry, it's just...

MIGUEL. Yes. You, on the other hand, look great.

SANDY. I look old.

MIGUEL. No.

SANDY. Fat.

MIGUEL. Please. Radiant. Radiant.

SANDY. Thank you.

MIGUEL. Your hair... it's uh... much smaller. You remember?

SANDY. Are you kidding? I was like... attack of the frizz.

MIGUEL. Come in. Please.

SANDY. I didn't know, when I spoke to you on the phone if it was okay to go out, or...

MIGUEL. ...if I was bedridden? Confined to quarters?

SANDY. I didn't know.

MIGUEL. I can go out. There's a coffee place down the street. Okay?

SANDY. Okay.

ASYMMETRY

(JULIUS re-emerges, towel in hand, and crosses to the bathroom.)

MIGUEL. Yes?
SANDY. Yes.
MIGUEL. Let me just get my coat... and... make yourself comfortable.

(As MIGUEL EXITS to the bedroom, JULIUS ENTERS the PRISCILLA-occupied bathroom. SANDY has a seat on the couch.)

JULIUS. Priscilla, I forgot to-

(PRISCILLA screams.)

PRISCILLA. Get out of here! Ohmygod!
JULIUS. *(Overlapping.)* Oh shit! I'm sorry, I thought-
PRISCILLA. What are you doing?!
JULIUS. Towel! I thought that you didn't have-
PRISCILLA. *(Overlapping.)* Have a towel, thank you!
JULIUS. I'm sorry, did you bring one, because-
PRISCILLA. *(Overlapping.)* What are you trying to do?!
JULIUS. If you need another one, then-
PRISCILLA. *(Overlapping.)* No, please.
JULIUS. I didn't see anything!
PRISCILLA. Please!
JULIUS. Okay?
PRISCILLA. Get out!
JULIUS. I didn't see any of your-
PRISCILLA. *(Overlapping.)* Ohmygod, get out. OUT!

ASYMMETRY

JULIUS. -parts.

(JULIUS tosses the towel into the bathroom and then retreats into the main room. He struggles to think of something to say that might diffuse the tension.)

JULIUS. I didn't see anything.
PRISCILLA. How can I know that?
JULIUS. I swear! Please, I thought I could just put it on the rack.
PRISCILLA. Just getting me a towel, that's all?
JULIUS. Yes. I mean, are you kidding, we just met... I'll be out here if you need anything.
PRISCILLA. Thank you.

(JULIUS sits at the table as MIGUEL re-emerges from the bedroom with his coat. He picks up his keys from the bar and thumbs through the meager cash left in his wallet.)

SANDY. My treat.
MIGUEL. No, I can take care of it.
SANDY. No, no, please... Miguel, I know how expensive...
MIGUEL. Coffee is? I can take care of it.
SANDY. It's no problem. With everything you've got-
MIGUEL. It's fine.
SANDY. *(Overlapping.)* -going on with the-
MIGUEL. *(Overlapping.)* No. Okay? We're not going to do that. You always wanted to pay your share. Your share isn't good enough anymore?
SANDY. It's enough.

(He crosses past her to the door, but stops before opening it.)

ASYMMETRY

MIGUEL. These games of 'I'll pay - no, please I insist.' They're beneath us, don't you think?

SANDY. Yes.

MIGUEL. So it's my treat.

(She punches his arm playfully.)

MIGUEL. Ow. You should watch it. I'm a sick man.

SANDY. You watch it.

(He waits for her to leave in front of him. PRISCILLA emerges from the bathroom wearing a dress.)

PRISCILLA. Julius?

JULIUS. Yes?

PRISCILLA. You ready?

JULIUS. Yes.

PRISCILLA. *(Sheepishly presenting herself.)* Okay.

JULIUS. You look great.

PRISCILLA. Right.

JULIUS. Totally.

PRISCILLA. If I had had time... you know... to get ready.

JULIUS. You look great.

PRISCILLA. Okay.

JULIUS. Hey, you remember that game we played with JackDaddy and OneEyedSix?

PRISCILLA. Which one?

JULIUS. The one where I drew like straight, straight, flush, full house, and everyone was all 'You hacked it! You totally hacked it!'

PRISCILLA. You were lucky.

ASYMMETRY

JULIUS. Yeah, that's what I was trying to say. That's how I feel tonight. I feel lucky.

PRISCILLA. Aww...

JULIUS. Yeah.

PRISCILLA. Because you saw me naked?

JULIUS. Your feet! I saw your feet naked!

PRISCILLA. You know, you really don't have to try to so hard.

JULIUS. Are you kidding?

PRISCILLA. It would be next to impossible for me to change my flight. I'm here for two days irregardless of your masculine charms.

JULIUS. You know... first of all, irregardless - not a word. Second-

PRISCILLA. Sure it is...

JULIUS. Second, I'm not... you know... going to spend time in the penalty box for trying to say something-

PRISCILLA. *(Overlapping.)* Irregardless, you've never heard of that?

JULIUS. I've heard of it. It's like unnecessary...

PRISCILLA. I know what it means.

JULIUS. *(Rushing to make his point.)* What I'm saying is: I'm not spending time in the penalty box-

PRISCILLA. *(Overlapping.)* Like- I intend to like my host

JULIUS. *(Overlapping.)* -for saying something nice.

PRISCILLA. ...irregardless of his faults.

JULIUS. Regardless! The word you're looking for is regardless. Regardless of his faults. I-R is completely unnecessary! Irregardless: It's like regardless for stupid people.

(PRISCILLA is furious. JULIUS immediately tries to placate her.)

ASYMMETRY

JULIUS. *(Cont.)* Shitfire. Shit! Shit! Shit! Shit! Shit! I'm sorry. I'm sorry, okay? I didn't mean to imply that...

PRISCILLA. I'm stupid?

JULIUS. No. Scout's honor. Totally didn't. Look, you know how they say I'm sorry in Italy? Linguini! A big-a plate a linguini.

PRISCILLA. *(Digging her heels in.)* I'm not sure I'll be comfortable in a fancy restaurant.

JULIUS. Oh, really, c'mon, you look great.

PRISCILLA. Julius...

JULIUS. I'm sorry. Adequate. Completely and totally adequate for a night on the town.

PRISCILLA. I always feel like waiters are judging me.

JULIUS. The waiter's are just as afraid of you as you are of them. They're not going to judge you. Besides I tip well. They all know me. I come in, they say: Bonjourno! Julius!

PRISCILLA. *(Suddenly territorial.)* Who do you take there?

JULIUS. I've never been. *(Catching Priscilla's hesitation.)* I'll make you a peanut butter sandwich, okay? You say we don't go, we don't go. Are you saying we don't go? Look, it'll be fun, I promise. It's just, I planned something. You know how big that is for me, right? I called, I made a reservation. Printed a map. Bought a shirt. Remember when you said... in the poker room, you said, I could never date you - you never leave your apartment. Well... I thought, okay, Julius, she's kind of got you there. But when you agreed to come out, I thought: I'll show her. I'll take her outside. I'll make a reservation, and then she'll... you know...

PRISCILLA. Julius. What do you think this is?

JULIUS. Do we have to define it?

PRISCILLA. I just don't want you to get the wrong idea-

ASYMMETRY

JULIUS. *(Cutting her off.)* It's nothing, okay? Mutual mastication.

PRISCILLA. Okay.

JULIUS. *(Offering her a jacket.)* Just a man and a woman in a loose spatial relationship.

(PRISCILLA shows her his acquiescence by taking the jacket.)

PRISCILLA. No physical stuff yet?
JULIUS. Yet?
PRISCILLA. *(Exiting.)* Yet.
JULIUS. Sweet. I mean, yeah, totally.

(After PRISCILLA EXITS, CODY and MAGGIE burst onstage through the front door. MAGGIE has her legs wrapped around CODY's waist and she kisses him furiously as he stumbles into her apartment.)

JULIUS. *(Cont.)* Hottest this evening gets is right now.

(JULIUS EXITS behind the amorous couple and closes the door behind him simultaneously with MAGGIE flinging it shut. CODY looks around for a place to lie her down. The couch will do.)

CODY. You left your lights on.
MAGGIE. Shut up.

(Their hands are all over each other as they dance their way towards sex. CODY kisses her from her neck down to her belly, lifting her shirt up just enough to expose skin. MAGGIE grabs his head and pulls him back up.)

ASYMMETRY

MAGGIE. Oh! Holy shit!
CODY. What?
MAGGIE. I fucking love this!

(CODY's about to mumble an affirmation, but she kisses him again, then bites his lower lip.)

CODY. Ow! You bit me!

(He looks down at her, surprised, but no less excited.)

MAGGIE. Oops. C'mere, I won't hurt you.

(He presses himself into her again and she bites his lip again.)

CODY. Jesus. I'm dreaming, right?
MAGGIE. I'll pinch you.
CODY. You can't actually exist, can you?

(She pinches him.)

CODY. Ow.
MAGGIE. You couldn't make me up.

(He hoists her up off the couch.)

MAGGIE. *(Laughing.)* Whoah.
CODY. Where's the bedroom?
MAGGIE. Ohmygod.

(CODY carries her off towards the bathroom.)

ASYMMETRY

CODY. Here?

MAGGIE. Bathroom, bathroom.

CODY. Oh.

MAGGIE. Put me down. Hold on, I need to check something first.

(MAGGIE lets him set her down and down and then disappears back into the bedroom, maintaining eye contact with him until she shuts the door.

CODY clenches his fists and mouths 'Holy Shit' in disbelief at his own good fortune. MAGGIE re-emerges with a bottle of scotch and two high ball glasses.)

MAGGIE. I–don't have any ice.

CODY. You want more to drink?

MAGGIE. Impatient?

CODY. Whatever.

MAGGIE. Say when... .

(She tips the bottle over the edge of the glass and leaves it there for a second before pouring.)

CODY. When. What year is this?

MAGGIE. *(Filling her own glass.)* They didn't tell me at Albertson's.

CODY. A toast.

MAGGIE. Ssuurre.

CODY. To... new friends.

MAGGIE. Uh-uh.

CODY. We can't be friends?

ASYMMETRY

MAGGIE. I think we'd make terrible friends.
CODY. Why would you say that...?
MAGGIE. I'd spend all my time wanting to fuck you.
CODY. *(Playing it cool.)* Okay.

(MAGGIE laughs at him trying to play it casual.)

CODY. What?
MAGGIE. To new lovers. How's that?
CODY. Yeah.

(Glasses clink.)

CODY. So... Maggie... what is it you didn't want me to see in your room?
MAGGIE. A girl can't want a drink?
CODY. No, that's cool.
MAGGIE. It's a mess.
CODY. You weren't expecting anyone?
MAGGIE. Not on a first date.
CODY. You know if you don't want to... it's okay...
MAGGIE. Want to what?
CODY. You know...
MAGGIE. What?
CODY. Go back and...
MAGGIE. Do the hokey-pokey? Play chess? C'mon. You can say it. Ohmygod, you're all red. Cody, are you serious?
CODY. Whatever.
MAGGIE. Cody?
CODY. I can say it. Have sex. 'Scool.
MAGGIE. M-hmm.
CODY. I thought maybe you were having... an outbreak.

ASYMMETRY

(MAGGIE'S demeanor changes instantaneously.)

MAGGIE. I'm not.

CODY. It would be okay, if you were. I mean, of course I would understand.

MAGGIE. *(Terse.)* I appreciate that.

CODY. I'm sorry... did I step in something?

MAGGIE. I don't want to talk about.

CODY. You don't have to be ashamed with me.

MAGGIE. Ohhhh, fuck that. Fuck that! Fuck being ashamed. You know how many of us would test positive for the herpes titer? One in six. Forty five million of us, laughing at the same Valtrex commercial, hoping no one will know.

CODY. That seems high.

MAGGIE. *(Overlapping.)* The doctor didn't give you the brochure?

CODY. That whole week was a blur.

MAGGIE. Tell me about it. I'm done being ashamed. You know what I did the whole week after? I took baths. I laid there in my bath tub, trying to feel clean.

CODY. I remember you saying that.

MAGGIE. What do you mean?

CODY. Nothing, I just...

MAGGIE. We weren't chatting then.

CODY. It was a post. On the message board.

MAGGIE. How long had you fucking been... you were lurking?

CODY. Uhhh...

MAGGIE. Oh my god, I hate lurkers. Reading everybody else's intimate secrets...

CODY. I'll tell you anything you want to know now.

ASYMMETRY

MAGGIE. What are you afraid of, more than anything?
CODY. Failure. I don't know. Love, I guess.
MAGGIE. I'm afraid of snakes. Love, really?
CODY. I should have said spiders?
MAGGIE. No, that's interesting. You want more Scotch?
CODY. I don't think so.
MAGGIE. Why?
CODY. It could hinder performance.
MAGGIE. Really? Optimistic?
CODY. Like you could resist.
MAGGIE. Ooooh. You're probably right.
CODY. Not sure it would be very smooth to get drunk and
pass out on you couch. Though it's a nice-

*(MAGGIE jumps on his back and he crashes forward into the
 couch.)*

MAGGIE. AAAAAhhhh!
CODY. Oh shit!
MAGGIE. Get it!
CODY. Jesus.

*(She lies on top of him, kissing the back of his neck
 aggressively.)*

CODY. Holy shit.
MAGGIE. See. It's very comfortable.
CODY. The couch?

(She bites Cody's ear lobe.)

CODY. *(Cont.)* Ow.

ASYMMETRY

MAGGIE. I keep wanting to bite you. Is that bad?
CODY. If you want there to be any of me left.
MAGGIE. I like it here.
CODY. On my back?
MAGGIE. Is this what it's like being a man? Getting behind a woman? Holding her down and...

(She rocks her hips backwards and forwards, pretending that she's a man. Cody's initial excitement give way to discomfort.)

MAGGIE. Giving it too her? Oh yeah...
CODY. *(Struggling to turn over.)* Umm...
MAGGIE. Get it.

(He turns over and looks up at her. She has him pinned by the shoulders.)

MAGGIE. You don't like that?
CODY. Not so much.
MAGGIE. *(Grabbing his crotch.)* Really?
CODY. I can't help that.
MAGGIE. I think you do. *(CODY runs a hand up the back of MAGGIE's leg.)*
MAGGIE. Checking to see if I shaved my legs?
CODY. No, but... uh... I'm delighted to see that you have. Or that you utterly hairless. Either's cool, you know.
MAGGIE. Are you? Utterly hairless?
CODY. No.
MAGGIE. Too hairy?
CODY. No... totally not hairy.
MAGGIE. Let's see.

ASYMMETRY

(She takes his shirt off and flings it upstage of the couch.)

MAGGIE. Ooooh.

CODY. I manscape a little. So it's... you know. All good. *(Pause.)* So, you know...

MAGGIE. Yeah?

CODY. I've shown you mine.

(He goes for her shirt unsuccessfully.)

MAGGIE. I should send you on your way. Let you masturbate tonight. Thinking of me.

CODY. That wouldn't be any fun for you.

MAGGIE. That's true.

(He goes to lift her again. She squirms out of his arms.)

MAGGIE. You wait. When I say, you can come in, okay?

CODY. You're killing me. *(Throws up his hands.)* All right.

MAGGIE. When I say, okay?

CODY. Okay.

(MAGGIE gets to upstage door and closes it most of the way, staring at CODY the whole time. When she's satisfied he'll wait forever, she beckons.)

MAGGIE. Okay, you can come in.

(She greets him at the door and kisses him when he crosses the-threshold. He closes the door behind him. MIGUEL and SANDY ENTER through the front door.)

MIGUEL. Here we are, back at my lair...

SANDY. Yes we are.

MIGUEL. Can I take your coat?

SANDY. Sure. You know, I think you're a much neater person than you were when we were...

MIGUEL. You think so...?

SANDY. Or did you just clean for me?

MIGUEL. Busted.

SANDY. This place is much cleaner than the house you guys had on Meridian.

MIGUEL. *That* was a nice place.

SANDY. I don't know how you could stand it.

MIGUEL. What?

SANDY. Rows and rows of dirty pipes...

MIGUEL. The bracing smell of marijuana and man-stink.

SANDY. I remember.

MIGUEL. Our minds were in the ether. We didn't have time for normal people things. Like... cleaning.

SANDY. *(Overlapping on 'cleaning')* Cleaning?

MIGUEL. Yes.

SANDY. You always made time for other things.

MIGUEL. Like...?

SANDY. Like women. Always two or three undergraduate women...

MIGUEL. There were three of us, you know. *(Sandy is skeptical.)* I haven't seen Havers in ages. And Jeff... You remember how Jeff would spend the last hour of every party asking everyone if they wanted to be part of his orgy?

SANDY. Those must have been some lonely orgies.

MIGUEL. You'd be surprised.

SANDY. God. *(Catching on.)* Oh God.

ASYMMETRY

MIGUEL. Mercy, please. *(Pause.)* I met his wife last year. Jeff and Mara Utley. He's a consultant now. Whatever that is. Hasn't picked up a pen in ten years. Most of them are like that. Rolling their eyes conspiratorially, like 'what were we thinking- poetry?'

SANDY. I didn't care for Jeff.

MIGUEL. Ah.

SANDY. Well...

MIGUEL. I didn't listen to Jeff, you know. Really.

SANDY. I'm sorry.

MIGUEL. His advice, if you could call it that...

SANDY. I'm not mad.

MIGUEL. Ah.

SANDY. Anymore. Miguel... I didn't come here to talk about the past...

MIGUEL. Please. Indulge me. One more story.

SANDY. Do I know it?

MIGUEL. I think. It's a night on the Meridian. Stars. We're on the roof. And you ask me for a poem. Extemporary. But I say, I have one already, Sandy Brown. I've had one memorized since our first class together.

SANDY. I know it.

MIGUEL. How did it go?

SANDY. You've forgotten...

MIGUEL. *(Reciting.)* I had a glimpse today
　　　　　Of wonderful Imperfection
　　　　　A smile that's not quite right
　　　　　A crooked smirk,
　　　　　A 'yeah, right, don't look at me'

　　　　　But I've seen it now
　　　　　And every hour I waste

ASYMMETRY

> Amidst perfect mouths in perfect light
> I'm lost in it
> The sweet, flawed smile of Sandy
> *(Referring to her smile.)* And there it is...

SANDY. It's too easy.

MIGUEL. I've missed you.

SANDY. Really? I was surprised you hadn't forgotten who I was.

MIGUEL. Are you kidding?

SANDY. I thought...

MIGUEL. That you were just one of many. No. I'm not the person you imagine I am, you know. You think - now I teach - that there must still be a long string of undergraduate women? No. It's just me. And this couch. And this table, and... *(Referring to sofa chair.)* ...that thing. A night after night Jeff Utley orgy with Sears. *(Pause.)* I remember you.

SANDY. I remember... *(Pause.)* Can... I use your facilities?

MIGUEL. Of course.

SANDY. Where...

MIGUEL. Turn around. *(As she leaves.)* Forgive the smell.

(As soon she's out of sight, MIGUEL grabs a prescription bottle of erectile dysfunction pills from the bedroom, then pours himself a glass of scotch. As the toilet flushes, he pops the pill into his mouth and takes a swig.)

SANDY. *(Re-emerging from the bathroom.)* Is drinking good for you?

MIGUEL. No.

SANDY. Your bathroom is a mess. You really need someone here to take care of you.

MIGUEL. Oh, you're volunteering?

SANDY. You couldn't afford me.

MIGUEL. You finish it. I insist. Aged twenty three years.

SANDY. Serendipitous.

MIGUEL. I might have well have the best. So... how would you answer the question?

SANDY. The question.

MIGUEL. "I haven't the heart, I haven't the soul, I haven't the divinity-"

SANDY. Stop it.

MIGUEL. What?

SANDY. You're making fun.

MIGUEL. I was remembering that day. Most honest thing you ever wrote in my class.

SANDY. I haven't written a word in twenty-two years.

MIGUEL. I'm sorry.

SANDY. Yes.

MIGUEL. So you're a nurse...?

SANDY. And a mother.

MIGUEL. Two point five kids?

SANDY. Two.

MIGUEL. You know, those things don't disqualify you.

SANDY. I haven't... the time. It's not something I would expect you to understand.

MIGUEL. Ah.

SANDY. You don't.

MIGUEL. I do. It's Newton's first law of motion.

SANDY. I think it's the 'external force' that's gotten to me.

MIGUEL. You want to know what I tell my students, when they feel like they're having trouble-

SANDY. *(Overlapping.)* No. I'm sorry.

ASYMMETRY

MIGUEL. Don't be.

SANDY. I'm not the person you imagine either.

MIGUEL. Yes, you are.

SANDY. No.

MIGUEL. Forgive me. I'm not your teacher anymore. *(Patting the couch.)* Please. Come sit.

(She sits on the sofa chair.)

SANDY. What about you?

MIGUEL. My work's taken a bit of a darker tone of late.

SANDY. Yes.

MIGUEL. Miguel Montes' ruminations on death, number 41. Very insightful, if you get that far.

SANDY. Listen, Miguel...

MIGUEL. No. I'm sorry, I don't want to do that, either.

SANDY. Are they sure? I've seen cases of pancreatic cancer-

MIGUEL. *(Cutting her off.)* Yes. Yes. Can I ask something of you?

SANDY. Of course.

MIGUEL. Come up to the roof with me.

SANDY. But... it's cold.

MIGUEL. I'll be fine. Just wait. Hang on. Don't leave.

(MIGUEL hurries into his bedroom and re-emerges with his journal.)

MIGUEL. *(Cont.)* You'll understand better if I read it to you.

SANDY. Are you sure?

MIGUEL. I'll take a coat, Sandy Brown.

ASYMMETRY

SANDY. Can we even...?

MIGUEL. *(Kneeling in front of her.)* I mean... it's not the effect, but I go up there all the time. Please.

SANDY. All right.

MIGUEL. Is that coat going to be enough for you?

SANDY. Yes.

MIGUEL. *(Holding the door open for her.)* Are you sure? Because I'll take the comforter off the bed. Wrap you up in it like a crepe.

SANDY. *(Exiting.)* I'll be fine.

JULIUS. *(O.S.)* I don't know what you're worried about.

(JULIUS and PRISCILLA ENTER through the front door.)

PRISCILLA. Julius, I'm am so sorry.

JULIUS. La Casa de Julius. What?

PRISCILLA. *(Overlapping.)* I'm sorry. I'm so sorry.

JULIUS. It's okay. It's fine.

PRISCILLA. It's just there was all those people and the maitre d' and those-

JULIUS. *(Overlapping.)* It's fine, please.

PRISCILLA. *(Overlapping.)* -those people at the window...and those prices?

JULIUS. Don't worry about it.

PRISCILLA. Thirty five dollars for lasagna?

JULIUS. Mom's special lasagna. From Sicily.

PRISCILLA. *(Overlapping.)* Everyone was looking at me.

JULIUS. No. C'mon.

PRISCILLA. I know I what I saw, Julius.

JULIUS. Because of your shoes...?

PRISCILLA. What's wrong with my shoes?

JULIUS. Probably wasn't the right place.

PRISCILLA. I'm sorry.

JULIUS. No, please. I had a good time. We had-a the free bread. Did you have a good time?

PRISCILLA. You'll never be able to go back there again.

JULIUS. Oh, please. I hate it there.

PRISCILLA. No you don't.

JULIUS. I've only ever ordered over the phone. When I order delivery, I'll just disguise my voice, you know. Scuse, scuse, scuse but I'd like-a two plates a-spaghetti.

PRISCILLA. *(Done with the bad Italian.)* Okay.

JULIUS. Can I take your coat Miss Strickland?

PRISCILLA. Thank you.

JULIUS. So where do you like to go?

PRISCILLA. Movies. It's dark. It's dark and you can scrunch down in your seat.

JULIUS. You ever get that, when you're sitting in a movie and it's dark for so long that forget it's light outside? You're come out and you're like...

(JULIUS squints at an imaginary sun.)

PRISCILLA. Yeah. I like that.

JULIUS. We could go tomorrow.

PRISCILLA. I'm really, sorry, Julius. About the reservation.

JULIUS. Ah, please. *(Pointing to the bar.)* Hey, you want something to drink?

PRISCILLA. I don't really drink alcohol...

JULIUS. No c'mon, this isn't alcohol, it's like... what is this... scotch? See? Less than twenty-five percent alcohol.

PRISCILLA. And two glasses ready, I see.

JULIUS. Oh yeah, I'm a two fister. Usually, I drink alone,

I'm all... *(Mimes drinking from two glasses.)* Wah. Wah.

PRISCILLA. How was that again?

JULIUS. *(Reading the bottle's label to entice her.)* 'Goes down smooth'.

PRISCILLA. They say alcohol is a social lubricant. You know... you say and do things you wouldn't normally do.

(Pause.)

JULIUS. So, you want a glass, or...

PRISCILLA. *(Laughing.)* No!

JULIUS. C'mon.

(JULIUS gives the bottle of shake.)

JULIUS. *(Jaws theme.)* Bum-bum-bum-bum-bum-bum. Deedle-dee.

PRISCILLA. All right. One.

(JULIUS arranges the glasses, then tilts the bottle carefully over one of them.

From the bedroom, MAGGIE gives a tremendous moan as the first drop of scotch hits the glass.)

MAGGIE. Ohhhhhh!

PRISCILLA. That's a lot.

JULIUS. Too much?

(The sound of CODY and MAGGIE's sex spills from bedroom into the living room. MAGGIE's moans should come in a natural rhythm, a steady beat that underscores the onstage action. JULIUS and PRISCILLA are completely unaware

ASYMMETRY

of the sound.
The awkward lulls in their conversation are due to their own
  romantic incompetence.)

MAGGIE. Ohhhh.... Ohhhhh...
JULIUS. So...
PRISCILLA. Yeah?
MAGGIE. Ohhh god!

(JULIUS, unused to the kick of hard alcohol, coughs a little
  after he swallows.)

PRISCILLA. You okay? You getting a cold?
MAGGIE. Ohhhhh...
JULIUS. Oh, yeah, just a little, you know...
MAGGIE. Ohhhhh!
JULIUS. *(Steve McQueen:)* I'm just enjoying the taste.
MAGGIE. Oh!
JULIUS. That bread was good tonight.
MAGGIE. Oh!
PRISCILLA. Was good bread.
MAGGIE. Oh!
JULIUS. Excellent bread.
PRISCILLA. Excellent bread
MAGGIE. Oh, Jesus!
JULIUS. How's that treating you?
MAGGIE. Oh!
PRISCILLA. Good.
MAGGIE. Oh!
PRISCILLA. Ummm... I don't think it's having an effect
on me.
MAGGIE. FUCK!

ASYMMETRY

JULIUS. Really? I'm sorry, where are my manners? Have a seat.

(She sits on the couch and smiles at him. He takes on the takes a seat on the far side of the couch and stares in the opposite direction. MAGGIE's moans become louder as the two struggle for something to say.)

MAGGIE. Ohhhhhh, yeah... come and get it

(JULIUS slides over towards PRISCILLA.)

MAGGIE. *(Cont.)* Ohhhhh Jesus. Ohhhhhh. Ohhhhhh Jesus...

PRISCILLA. This stuff makes me sleepy.

MAGGIE. Oh...

JULIUS. Really, I'm totally wired.

MAGGIE. Oh...

JULIUS. Could go on all night.

MAGGIE. Oh...

JULIUS. You know me.

MAGGIE. Oh...

JULIUS. I'll get all the sleep I'll need when I'm...

MAGGIE. Oh...

JULIUS. you know...

MAGGIE. Oh...

JULIUS. ...tired.

MAGGIE. Ahn. Ahn. Ahn. Ahn. Ahn. Oh god. Yes! Fuckme, fuckme, fuckme, fuckme, fuckme.

JULIUS. *(Referring to the Scotch.)* This is good.

(PRISCILLA crosses her left leg over her right and leans away

ASYMMETRY

from him.)

MAGGIE. Ahn, ahn, ahn, ahn, ahn, ahn, ahn. C'mon, c'mon, c'mon, c'mon.

(JULIUS interprets the leg cross as an invitation and awkwardly slides across the couch and puts his arm behind the couch. He struggles to find a suave way to touch her.)

MAGGIE. Don't stop. Don't stop, Oh jesus, I'm coming, I'm com- I'm coming. Oh...

(He rests his hand awkwardly on her shoulder. It doesn't have the intended effect.)

PRISCILLA. Julius...
JULIUS. *(Brushing her shoulder.)* You have some lint on your shoulder pad. *(Pause.)* I'm sorry. I'm not good at this.
PRISCILLA. You don't have to be.
JULIUS. I'm sorry. I just wanted to... I just wanted to kiss you. I don't know how to do that. Do I ask you? Do I... I don't know... snatch you up in my arms...? And you know...?
PRISCILLA.No.
JULIUS. I mean, what? Do I like... grab your face?
PRISCILLA. No!
JULIUS. Or your shoulders. I don't know... you tell me what to do and I'll do it. Whatever hoops I have to jump through.
PRISCILLA. Is that what all this is about?
JULIUS. No! No, it's not. I can't talk without screwing up my own words. What I'm trying to say is...
PRISCILLA. *(Overlapping.)* I don't know why you're try-ing so hard.

ASYMMETRY

JULIUS. *(Overlapping.)* Is it okay if I kiss you? Because if it is, that's great. If not, that's great too. Not as great, but... you know... Can I? Please?

PRISCILLA. I thought we decided we would save the physical stuff. You know, a loose spatial relationship.

JULIUS. But you're freaking magical! Your dress and that hair... Now that you're here standing right in front of me it's a like a trillion times harder. Look at you...

PRISCILLA. Yes...?

JULIUS. *(Staring anywhere but her face.)* You're freaking...

PRISCILLA. My face. Julius. Up here.

JULIUS. *(Looking her in the eye.)* That too.

PRISCILLA. I don't understand.

JULIUS. What?

PRISCILLA. I don't why you're acting like this. Help me.

JULIUS. What?

PRISCILLA. I don't understand.

JULIUS. What do you mean? Priscilla?

PRISCILLA. Why you would...

JULIUS. What?

PRISCILLA. Why you would want me? Are you desperate? Do you have a blind spot?

JULIUS. No.

PRISCILLA. What then? I thought maybe you would get to know me... you know... spend this whole weekend and then maybe, but after a few drinks...

JULIUS. You think it's the alcohol? You think I have goggles on?

PRISCILLA. Do you?

JULIUS. No. God. You think I'm like after your money or something?

ASYMMETRY

PRISCILLA. No.

JULIUS. ...or I'm some kind of weird fetish guy?

PRISCILLA. No.

JULIUS. I know you already, that's all. And you know me. And that's why you're out here, all the way from Denver. Not to see San Jose on some random weekend trip. You want to see San Jose? It's like boom, there's the Winchester Mystery House. There's the light rail. I can show you San Jose - I'll just walk outside, point to the nearest windowed office building and say, 'see, it all looks like that.' You came out to see me... right? Didn't you? You came out here hoping there might be something, you know, something... because we're two people who play too much online poker- you know we played like two hands an hour, you and me... because we'd chat and you'd be like: I wish there were men like you out here. You know. Single. Available. Compassionate. Right? *(She nods.)* And I said: I wish there were women like you out here because then, that would be something, you know someone who gets me, doesn't think that I'm a spazz or some kind of repulsively nice, asexual eunuch. I mean, that's the point, I already know you. You came out and you look different than I imagined, but I updated my mental picture and now I close my eyes and I attach you. So I know you. And I know that you wouldn't be out here if you didn't think you knew me too.

PRISCILLA. I know you.

JULIUS. Good.

PRISCILLA. I'm just afraid.

JULIUS. Of what?

PRISCILLA. I'm afraid that maybe you feel things I'm not capable of.

JULIUS. Like:

PRISCILLA. Like...

ASYMMETRY

JULIUS. Just try...

PRISCILLA. I'm not comfortable.

JULIUS. Open up and let me-

PRISCILLA. *(Overlapping.)* I'm not comfortable yet.

JULIUS. I'm not going to hurt you.

PRISCILLA. *(Overlapping.)* No, please. I have to go slow, Julius. Do you understand? I'm not comfortable. I'm not comfortable yet. Okay? I don't feel what you're feeling yet. I'm sorry. God. I'm sorry.

JULIUS. Okay. Yeah.

PRISCILLA. Okay?

JULIUS. Sure.

PRISCILLA. Don't be mad.

JULIUS. I'm not mad. I'm fine.

(He sits on the coffee table.)

PRISCILLA. Please don't be mad.

(She joins him.)

JULIUS. I'm fine. *(Pause.)* Hey, I'm making Denver omelets in the morning. You know... in honor of your homeland. You know... *(Great chieftain.)* 'we bring onions and green peppers to this sacred place... called Denver'

PRISCILLA. Julius. Thank you.

(She reaches out and touches his arm.)

JULIUS. Yeah. Hey, you know. Yeah. That's uh...

PRISCILLA. Thank you.

JULIUS. Hey look, I want you to sleep in my bed tonight.

No. No! Not like that. I mean, I'll sleep on the couch. You sleep on the bed. You're jet lagged, you're tired. You take the bed. Please.

PRISCILLA. I'm fine on the couch.

JULIUS. I insist.

PRISCILLA. Okay. *(Pointing to the bedroom.)* Do you mind if I...

JULIUS. No, please.

PRISCILLA. The alcohol made me sleepy.

JULIUS. Not a problem. I'll probably... you know watch some TV or something. Hey, sleep well.

PRISCILLA. *(Opening the door to the bedroom.)* Thanks.

JULIUS. Big day tomorrow. On the town.

PRISCILLA. Okay. Good night.

(After watching her leave, JULIUS sits himself down on the SL side of the couch and props his head against his arm. MAGGIE comes out of her bedroom a few moments later, wrapped in a blanket and plops down on the SR side of the couch. She props her head on her right arm, in opposition to JULIUS. While MAGGIE curls up on the couch and gets ready to sleep, JULIUS is struck with a sudden inspiration. He gets up off the couch, throws on a coat and exits through the front door.

CODY emerges from the bedroom, wearing only his boxer shorts.)

CODY. Shit, I fell asleep.

MAGGIE. It's all right. You're fine.

CODY. You all right?

MAGGIE. Look at you in those boxers. Hot.

CODY. *(Pulling down his waistband.)* I can... take them

off again.

MAGGIE. Nope.

CODY. Why are you out here?

MAGGIE. I have trouble sleeping next to people.

CODY. Oh. Shit, I'm sorry. Anybody?

MAGGIE. Anybody but my brother.

CODY. Do you want me to leave?

MAGGIE. No, you're fine. I said you're fine. Who'll make me breakfast?

CODY. I should probably tell you...

MAGGIE. Who'll *get* me breakfast?

CODY. I'm your man.

MAGGIE. Yes you are.

(Pause.)

CODY. That was great, by the way. Did I say that?

MAGGIE. Yes. You were like 'that was very good...'

(She trails off and snores.)

CODY. I sleep after sex.

MAGGIE. Uh-huh.

CODY. I was very tired.

MAGGIE. Uh-huh.

CODY. *(Grabbing his shirt.)* You'll learn this about me.

MAGGIE. Optimism again.

CODY. Confidence. Hey, I've been you know... *(Flexing.)* ...working out a little lately. You don't think I'm getting too big, do you?

MAGGIE. No.

CODY. *(Throwing his shirt on.)* You're sure you're okay

out here?

(MAGGIE stares downstage, unfulfilled and anxious.)

MAGGIE. I'm fine.
CODY. Okay. I'll be uhh... Goodnight.

(CODY exits back to the bedroom and shuts the door.)

(SANDY ENTERS from the front door and floats to the couch. She leans against it, facing upstage. MIGUEL steps in into the apartment, regarding her. The long study makes her uncomfortable and she slides around the couch.)

MIGUEL. ...and silence falls.
SANDY. I should go.
MIGUEL. There's the door.
SANDY. You wouldn't mind? I mean...
MIGUEL. What you do-
SANDY. I mean, you wouldn't be hurt-
MIGUEL. *(Overlapping.)* ...that's entirely up to you. But.. but... there is another door.
SANDY. Which leads to...
MIGUEL. Tonight.

(He closes on her.)

SANDY. No, I mean...
MIGUEL. I haven't the luxury.

(His kisses her. She breaks it off, desperate to keep things conversational. She fails. He kisses her again. She breaks

ASYMMETRY

it off.)

SANDY. Wait. Wait.

(Temporarily thwarted, he doesn't let go completely. He keeps hold of her hand and flips it over. He runs his finger up her forearm.)

SANDY. Oh... wait. You said...
MIGUEL. Yes?
SANDY. You said in your...
MIGUEL. I'm listening.
SANDY. You said in your poem: 'only my shadow will mourn me'. What did you mean...?

(He stops and lays her hand back down at her side.)

MIGUEL. *(Going directly to the Scotch bottle.)* I thought you would understand better if I read it.
SANDY. I love your words.
MIGUEL. They won't keep you warm. *(Pause.)* It's about legacy.
SANDY. And you think everything dies with you?
MIGUEL. You know, I haven't given it much thought.
SANDY. I don't believe you.
MIGUEL. What do you want?
SANDY. I wanted to say something. To you.
MIGUEL. Ah.
SANDY. It would be so easy for me to fall for you again, Miguel.
MIGUEL. And you're afraid of that?
SANDY. No, I'm afraid that you might not be around.

ASYMMETRY

(Pause.)

MIGUEL. I don't want to talk about it. I don't want talk about it, I don't want to think about it. This thing sits in my stomach... and then for a second, for an evening with you... it's gone. If I have a six months left, three months, I'd rather spend them forgetting...

SANDY. I understand.

MIGUEL. You're no different than you were, you know that?

SANDY. Yes I am.

MIGUEL. Your eyes crinkle a little more when you smile.

SANDY. Among other things.

MIGUEL. No.

SANDY. What?

MIGUEL. I won't have you disparage what I love. *(Reaching for her hair clip.)* May I...?

(Slowly, MIGUEL removes the clip from SANDY's hair and unfurls her long hair. He gently lets it drop to the sides of her face and runs his fingers through it. She pulls a clump in front of her face to hide from his penetrating gaze. He pulls it back, refusing to let the moment pass.)

MIGUEL. Exactly the same.

SANDY. No, I'm not. I... uh...

MIGUEL. Yes?

SANDY. It would be so easy to fall for you again.

(She kisses him. He leads her back towards the bedroom. Stops before the threshold and kisses her again.

ASYMMETRY

*CODY ENTERS and crosses to the couch. He checks to see if
MAGGIE is asleep. Her eyes open as soon as he kneels
next to her.)*

MAGGIE Cody...?
CODY. I can't sleep.
MAGGIE. You're seriously not tired?
CODY. Had a nap. I'm ready for uhh. .
MAGGIE. No.
CODY. The sex.
MAGGIE. Really?
CODY. No, I'm just kidding.
MAGGIE. It hurts.
CODY. I'm sorry-
MAGGIE. You were a little...
CODY. *(Simultaneously with above.)* -I was a little... exu-
berant?

(MIGUEL leads Sandy into the bedroom.)

MAGGIE. It's fine.
CODY. Its just... it's so great, you know. Don't you think?
You were saying before, but...
MAGGIE. Yes.
CODY. No strings attached. I mean, can you even remem-
ber? I'm sorry, were you trying to sleep out here?
MAGGIE. It's fine.
CODY. You ever think that...
MAGGIE. Yes...?
CODY. It's dumb. Did you ever think like... maybe... you'd
have to give up like finding that one person?
MAGGIE. *(Laughing.)* What?

ASYMMETRY

CODY. You know, like maybe I have... you know...

MAGGIE. Herpes?

CODY. Yeah. So maybe when I meet miss right and she'd be disgusted and that would be that. Totally rot something that was meant to be. End up settling for someone that tolerates you. You'd never felt like that?

MAGGIE. No.

CODY. I guess. If it's meant to be... Right.

MAGGIE. I stopped believing there was a special someone that day Brian Halstrom rolled over me to throw his condom away. Jesus, really?

CODY. I said, that's how I felt.

MAGGIE. You thought that somehow, in this fucked-up planet that the two of you would be drawn together, like magnetic north and magnetic south? What if she was born in the Ukraine? You think you'd find each other?

CODY. No.

MAGGIE. Through snow and sleet. Jesus.

CODY. The Ukraine?

MAGGIE. I think my someone got hit by a bus. Wham! Now what am I supposed to do?

CODY. Find yourself a man-toy, I guess. *(Flexing.)* You know... someone a little buffed.

MAGGIE. You know where...?

CODY. You'll see.

(Pause.)

MAGGIE. You know what I think? Love at first sight, soul mates... just a magic way to explain basic human instinct. You don't agree?

CODY. I don't know.

ASYMMETRY

MAGGIE. When you look at another person you're saying: 'do I want to carry that person's genes?' Is this the right
mate? Can he provide for me and our unborn children?

CODY. That's what you were thinking?

MAGGIE. I'm not kidding.

CODY. This is what they're teaching at San Jose State?

MAGGIE. You're a scientist.

CODY. Environmental chemist.

MAGGIE. What do you think makes women-

CODY. *(Overlapping.)* I study water samples.

MAGGIE. What do you think makes women attractive?

CODY. I don't know. *(Describing her.)* Let's see. Glasses.
Brown hair. Lazy smile.

*(CODY moves closer to her, eager to be closer to her... and to
be done with this conversation.)*

MAGGIE. I'm serious.

CODY. I don't know... Sense of humor?

MAGGIE. Right.

CODY. Intelligence.

MAGGIE. *(Buzzer sound.)* Errrrrr.

CODY. You're telling me what I like?

MAGGIE. Yeah.

CODY. I'm telling you...

MAGGIE. This isn't a Redbook survey.

CODY. ...what I like. Is there a wrong answer to this?

MAGGIE. There's a right answer. You ready for it?

CODY. All right.

MAGGIE. Men are looking for symmetry. Perfect facial
alignment-

CODY. Nah.

MAGGIE. There's been studies. You know: 'take a look at these pictures-

CODY. *(Overlapping.)* Yeah, but...

MAGGIE. -and tell us which one is more attractive'. Men also-

CODY. College hooey.

MAGGIE. Men also look for... hooey? Please. They also look for a perfect waist-to-hip ratio. You know why?

CODY. I don't care about the math of it.

MAGGIE. This is for your edification.

CODY. I'm not... Why?

MAGGIE. Everything... it's about genetic fitness. Human beings are so enlightened, right, we're so much better than everything else that crawls around the earth, but in the end we're still bound by the same laws. Same rules apply.

CODY. I don't believe that.

MAGGIE. You're going to tell me about... what? Bald Eagles? The Icelandic Albatross?

CODY. I don't know anything about the Icelandic Albatross. I was going to say, I don't buy it. I mean that's it?

MAGGIE. Yes.

CODY. Look at your face. One of your eyes is higher up than the other... should I run for the door?

MAGGIE. *(Going to the mirror.)* My eye isn't higher up.

CODY. Totally is.

MAGGIE. Bullshit.

CODY. I don't care-

MAGGIE. *(Overlapping.)* My eyes line up. That's fucking-

CODY. *(Overlapping.)* Listen. My point is: I don't care.

MAGGIE. You're just saying that, right? To make a point?

CODY. Maybe it's... we're all just looking for balance, you know... trying to find people who are fucked up in the opposite direction.

MAGGIE. There's empirical evidence.

CODY. I don't care.

MAGGIE. You don't care?

CODY. No. So what? A thousand years ago the earth was flat.

MAGGIE. The earth was never flat.

CODY. You know what I mean.

MAGGIE. You're a fucking scientist.

CODY. Yeah.

MAGGIE. So I say here's a mountain of... you know... facts to support my theory.

CODY. I'm talking about personal experience. I'm talking about, you have one eye higher than the other and I'm still totally attracted to you.

MAGGIE. Jesus, will you stop trying so hard? I'm not sleeping with you again.

CODY. I know. What, you mean ever?

MAGGIE. I'm saying: shut up about my fucking eye, all right?

CODY. All right. Damn.

(Pause.)

CODY. So that's your theory, then? About love and...?

MAGGIE. At least now you don't have to be afraid of it anymore. De-mystified.

CODY. Yeah. I'm much less confused.

MAGGIE. Fuck you. Is that what you're looking for?

CODY. Yes.

MAGGIE. Great.

CODY. And you're not?

ASYMMETRY

MAGGIE. That mean you're going to come around every so often and piddle on my porch?

CODY. No. Fuck.

MAGGIE. Did I make a boo-boo?

CODY. Please. Like you aren't looking for the same fucking thing.

MAGGIE. Happily ever after?

CODY. No. Just... you know...

MAGGIE. Jesus.

CODY. Love. Somebody. A warm body to sleep next to. Not just tonight but maybe every night.

MAGGIE. I told you.

CODY. I don't believe that.

MAGGIE. Yeah. You think I hate it so much I want it every night?

CODY. Maybe I do.

MAGGIE. I'm some kind of sadist?

CODY. Masochist, actually... but, sure. Everyone is a little.

MAGGIE. You fucking snore. You think I like that? You're hairy. This is the twenty first century, you ever hear of waxing? It's like fucking a chimp.

CODY. *(Losing the battle to keep his sense of humor.)* You said it was good...

MAGGIE. Yeah.

CODY. You said it was good...

MAGGIE. Listen Cody... the afterglow will fade, trust me.

CODY. Fuck that. Fuck that.

MAGGIE. *(Overlapping.)* I'm not most girls, all right?

CODY. This is... what?

MAGGIE. You don't have to stick around and talk or-

CODY. *(Overlapping.)* Some kind of chemical reaction?

MAGGIE. Maybe. Listen...

CODY. Fuck.

MAGGIE ...I release you. It's okay.

CODY. I don't want to...

MAGGIE. You can be a man this time, guilt free.

CODY. I don't want to.

MAGGIE. I'll call you.

CODY. Right.

(CODY slams his fist against the door to bedroom, causing it to fly open. He angrily collects his clothes.)

CODY. *(Cont.)* Look, I'm trying to understand how you can be all... you know... one minute and the next a total...

MAGGIE. Bitch? Why can't you say what you mean? Bitch?

CODY. *(Overlapping.)* Yeah, all right. A total fucking bitch.

MAGGIE. Fuck you.

CODY. I mean... is this what you want?

MAGGIE. What I want-

CODY. *(Overlapping.)* What are you afraid of?

MAGGIE. What I want is-

CODY. Maggie, please!

MAGGIE. What I want is for you to get the fuck out of my apartment!

CODY. I thought we had something, you know...

MAGGIE. What do I have to do? Call the fucking police?!

CODY. A connection, you know...

MAGGIE. Yeah, you stuck your dick in me.

CODY. A connection.

MAGGIE. I'll fucking call them. Please!

CODY. I thought, here's someone who gets me-

MAGGIE. Please.

CODY. Listen to me! Here's someone who gets me, some-one-

MAGGIE. No.

CODY. Someone who knows what it's like-

MAGGIE. Just go.

CODY. Hold on. Someone who knows what it's like to feel disgusting. And untouchable. And to have to dredge that up every first date, every time you get close to someone... And that look. That look that says 'there's no way I'm calling you now that you have herpes-

MAGGIE. *(Breaking down.)* GET OUT! GET OUT! GET THE FUCK OUT OF MY APARTMENT! GET OUT! Please... Please...

(Silence. CODY fights his instinct to stay and console her as she sobs. He finally grabs his clothes and heads for the door.)

MAGGIE. *(Stopping him.)* I'm sorry.

CODY. It's okay. Do you need...?

MAGGIE. I don't want to talk about it anymore.

CODY. Ok. Ok. Can I...?

MAGGIE. I'm fine.

MAGGIE. I feel too much. You ever get that?

CODY. Sometimes.

MAGGIE. I still feel like I have splinters... you know... Dug in there so deep that every time I take a deep breath I can feel them.

CODY. It's okay.

MAGGIE. Does that make sense?

CODY. Yeah.

MAGGIE. What did you like about me?

ASYMMETRY

CODY. Are you kidding?

MAGGIE. That's it?

CODY. No, no. I was going to say... here's someone who understands me, you know. Someone who gets what it's like.

MAGGIE. What if we could erase everything and start over... would you do it? Would you feel all of those things for the first time?

CODY. No.

MAGGIE. I would. Can you imagine? Love for the first time?

CODY. Yeah.

MAGGIE. Sex for the first time? Sex without guilt?

CODY. That's still possible.

MAGGIE. First kiss?

CODY. You're twenty-two, Maggie.

MAGGIE. I know.

CODY. You act like your life is over.

MAGGIE. Don't lecture me, okay?

CODY. I'm just saying there are a lot more firsts out there...

MAGGIE. Really?

CODY. Hey. C'mere.

(He holds her. It isn't what she wanted, but she doesn't resist.)

MAGGIE. Cody...

CODY. I could love you.

MAGGIE. *(Terse.)* No.

CODY. Maggie...

(MAGGIE tries to struggle out his grasp. CODY decides he's not going to let go this time.)

ASYMMETRY

MAGGIE. No. I didn't let you.
CODY. I'm not trying to...
MAGGIE. I want you to go.
CODY. C'mon.

(Her struggle to free herself becomes more desperate.)

CODY. Maggie, wait...
MAGGIE. Goddamnit! Let go of me!
CODY. I'm not going to leave you-
MAGGIE. Fuck! Let go!

(As soon as he lets go of her, she slaps him. Hard.)

MAGGIE. I didn't let you!

(For a split second, MAGGIE is unsure whether CODY will respond violently and she braces herself. His initial shock and anger give way to hurt and he retreats through the front door.
As MAGGIE crosses to the bar, JULIUS ENTERS and takes a miniature plastic castle out the brown paper bag and sets it on the coffee table. He lays down and looks at it, the cheap plastic toy he's bought.)

MIGUEL. *(Offstage.)* I said: Forget about it, all right?!
SANDY. *(Offstage.)* I said I don't care, Miguel,
MIGUEL. *(Offstage.)* I said forget about it!
SANDY. *(Offstage.)* I don't know why-
MIGUEL. *(Offstage.)* Oh, please! Please.

(MAGGIE EXITS to the bathroom carrying with a pipe and bag

of weed she had stored in the bar.)

SANDY. *(Offstage.)* It doesn't matter.

MIGUEL. *(Offstage.)* I matters, all right? The sex... You know what, nothing. Forget it. You want to sleep here, that's fine.

SANDY. Please don't walk away.

(Onstage, JULIUS opens the mini-draw bridge to the mini castle with his index finger. MAGGIE runs her finger around the edge of her scotch glass.

MIGUEL storms out of the room in his bathrobe, completely unaware of JULIUS. He paces back and forth his fists clenching and unclenching, a caged animal, ready to vent his frustration on the first human target. He pulls on his dick in frustration. Takes the bottle of pills from his robe pocket and flings them at the wall.)

MIGUEL. Fuck!

(SANDY appears in the doorway, frightened but resolute.)

SANDY. It isn't fair.

MIGUEL. You have cause to complain?

SANDY. It happens to every man.

MIGUEL. Really? And when it happens to everyman, does his woman condescend? Does he push his prick between his legs and beg for another chance?

SANDY. It doesn't matter.

MIGUEL. It matters! Of course it matters! What am I to you, now? Huh? What am I to you?! What? A lover? An artist? A dissonant voice? Who you worship? Because you did! You did. I saw your eyes then and I remember. All I am to you now is a cancer patient.

SANDY. No.

MIGUEL. A fucking cancer patient! How many do you see everyday? Do they clutch at your breast and beg for life? Forgiveness? Do you offer them a kind word before you clean their fucking bedpan? And now you want to take care of me?! Fuck you, Sandy Brown.

SANDY. Don't call me that.

MIGUEL. Of course.

SANDY. It isn't my name.

MIGUEL. Fine. Sandy Livingston. Where's the poetry in that?

SANDY. Miguel, why are wasting our time together fighting-

MIGUEL. Our time together ends the minute you dress and leave.

SANDY. Fine.

(She EXITS into the bedroom. MIGUEL takes another swallow of scotch. For moment, he seems on the verge of a complete emotional breakdown. His brief vulnerability ends when he decides he's more comfortable going back on the attack.)

MIGUEL. Hey Sandy? You ever think maybe it doesn't happen to every man? Sandy? You ever think maybe it only happens to every man who sleeps with you?

SANDY. *(Exiting the bedroom with her clothes.)* Why are you doing this?

MIGUEL. Maybe in all the foreplay, all the tender mercies, the gentle caresses- *(Miming dick going limp.)* -it all just goes to shit.

SANDY. You. Asshole.

MIGUEL. There it is!

SANDY. You. Goddamn. Asshole.

MIGUEL. It's like having sex with a nursery school teacher. Now roll over little-

SANDY. *(Overlapping.)* Please, Miguel! Please!

MIGUEL. -roll over little Miguel and let Miss Livingston shove her thumb up your ass. I swear I'm even limper now just thinking about.

(SANDY is in tears.)

MIGUEL. *(Cont.)* What you think you can just cry and I'm going to fall apart?! No, Sandy, it's really good technique... but if you're trying to manipulate someone, maybe you shouldn't turn away. Do you even remember who you were? I remember. I remember when you arched your back and you were loud. And you bit me. Softly at first and then when I smiled, a little harder. And a little harder still? You remember Alum Rock? The night on the meridian, the night that-

SANDY. Yes. I remember that night.

MIGUEL. Ah, yes. The wayward romance with the Cuban.

SANDY. No. You cheapened it. That was never-

MIGUEL. *(Overlapping.)* Oh, please.

SANDY. -me. That was never me.

MIGUEL. *(Overlapping.)* Please.

SANDY. *(Overlapping.)* You cheapened it! That was never me!

MIGUEL. I never lied to you.

SANDY. You lied to me every time you opened your mouth! You still lie!

MIGUEL. No.

SANDY. Every tenderness. Then and now.

MIGUEL. *(Overlapping.)* Don't talk to me about lying.

SANDY. Name one true thing-

MIGUEL. *(Overlapping.)* You lie to yourself with every breath. 'I haven't the -'

SANDY. Name one true thing you've said to me.

MIGUEL. *(Overlapping.)* What? I haven't the-

SANDY. One thing.

MIGUEL. I haven't the passion! You haven't the passion. And there it is. One true thing. You haven't the passion. You haven't the life.

SANDY. Thank you.

MIGUEL. What? Oh, no, don't leave yet. This is just getting fun.

SANDY. Go...

MIGUEL. Yes?

SANDY. Go... Fuck yourself!

MIGUEL. Yes!

SANDY. Go fuck yourself!

MIGUEL. I love it!

SANDY. I'm so glad this is fun for you!

MIGUEL. Yes!

SANDY. Fuck off!!!

MIGUEL. This is great, Sandy.

SANDY. I'm leaving.

MIGUEL. No, wait.

SANDY. Please.

MIGUEL. Say it again-

SANDY. No!

MIGUEL. Say it: Fuck!

SANDY. Asshole!

MIGUEL. No, wait. Sandy, what did you expect? You think

somehow this storybook romance ends well?

SANDY. Don't condescend to me, do you know how infuriating-

MIGUEL. *(Overlapping.)* Please, you invite it-

SANDY. -it is when you do that?

MIGUEL. *(Overlapping.)* You invite condescension with every breath.

SANDY. I think-

MIGUEL. Okay, yes-

SANDY. I think that you're.

MIGUEL. -can we skip to the end? I'm a bad person.

SANDY. I think that it's disgusting...

MIGUEL. Disgusting pig, yes, yes.

SANDY. The way you've ended up.

MIGUEL. No. We're not doing that.

SANDY. Disgusting.

MIGUEL. You don't judge me.

SANDY. You remember the sex, well enough, but do you remember anything else?

MIGUEL. What else was there?

SANDY. You were beautiful. Everything about you was beautiful. You cavorted and you lied but you were amazing. Just being near you. Everyone just wanted to be near you and they felt lucky. Yes. I worshipped you. Okay? Does that empower you?

MIGUEL. *(Retreating to the bar.)* No.

SANDY. And now...

MIGUEL. Everything ends badly. Isn't that clear enough for you, Sandy?

SANDY. Are you so desperate to have me pity you?

MIGUEL. *(Piqued.)* I want you to leave. Right now.

SANDY. All right.

MIGUEL. Why did you even come here?! What were you even hoping for? Closure? An end to the Miguel Montes chapter?

SANDY. No.

MIGUEL. One last chance to turn the tables?

SANDY. I came here to...

MIGUEL. To get back at your fucking husband?

SANDY. No.

MIGUEL. Your ex-husband then? Has he found someone?

SANDY. I never married.

MIGUEL. Ah. Scandalous.

SANDY. Yes.

MIGUEL. Children born into-

SANDY. *(Overlapping.)* Miguel...

MIGUEL. -a broken home.

SANDY. Don't you dare.

MIGUEL. Who was he?

SANDY. You want a story about us? A month after Jeff Utley and his advice, I'm sitting. At Rico's. Waiting for you. And then there you are. Smooth. Charming. An hour late. A hand on my knee. Fast friends, like nothing had happened and I still felt lucky to be next to you. Even though I hated you. I hated you. And you ordered beers, one right after the other. And said, no thanks, and then 'ah'. Oblivious. I sit on the razor's edge of my life. Between 'I'm pregnant' and 'Not thirsty.' See?

(Silence.)

SANDY. *(Cont.)* They look like you. You know that? Every day, they look like you. Maggie, she laughs like you. So I can't just leave and forget you. There's no closure.

ASYMMETRY

(Silence.)

SANDY. *(Cont.)* Maggie and Julius. Born January 9th, 1984. Just over ten months after...

MIGUEL. Yes. I get it.

SANDY. So when you asked if I remember that night-

MIGUEL. *(Overlapping.)* I get it.

SANDY. I came here because I thought maybe you'd... maybe you'd want to meet them. Julius, he's a networks consultant. No college, but... And Maggie, she's a student at San Jose State. Anthropology. Not poetry, but...

MIGUEL. I can't believe it.

SANDY. Oh... here!

MIGUEL. No please. I don't want to see that.

SANDY. But...

MIGUEL. I have a choice, don't I?

SANDY. Yes.

MIGUEL. I mean, now I have a choice?

SANDY. You'd rather I told you?

MIGUEL. Yes.

SANDY. Why?

MIGUEL. You ask me that?

SANDY. What would you have said?

MIGUEL. Not given the opportunity...

SANDY. Please.

MIGUEL. I would have said:

SANDY. Yes?

MIGUEL. Well, given the opportunity, I might have...

SANDY. *(Overlapping.)* What?

MIGUEL. I might have paid for the abortion.

(SANDY drops the picture of her children on the ground.)

MIGUEL. You see? I would have made an excellent father.

SANDY. Yes.

MIGUEL. No, seriously, Sandy, I would have saved them from their whole miserable lives.

SANDY. Goodbye.

MIGUEL. One more thing: When they ask you about me, what do you tell them?

SANDY. About you?

MIGUEL. Am I a pig? Have you poisoned our children against me?

SANDY. I tell them you're dead.

(She EXITS. MIGUEL looks at the picture lying on the ground, but, after a moment's consideration, he decides he's not interested and goes back into the bedroom.

PRISCILLA enters, carrying a yearbook, and heads towards the front door. Before she reaches it, her conscience gets the better of her and she crosses to the couch. She gently shakes Julius awake.)

JULIUS. What time is it?

PRISCILLA. It's midnight.

JULIUS. You can't sleep?

PRISCILLA. Julius. I'm leaving.

JULIUS. *(Standing.)* What? Why?

PRISCILLA. I'm sorry, I have to.

JULIUS. No wait. Priscilla. I'm sorry about earlier, okay? I made a total mess, okay?

PRISCILLA. It's not that.

JULIUS. What?

PRISCILLA. I found this.

ASYMMETRY

(She hands him the yearbook.)

JULIUS. My yearbook?

PRISCILLA. I remember you. Julius Livingston Seagull. I signed your yearbook.

JULIUS. So?

PRISCILLA. *(Reading.)* 'Seagull- hope you forgive me for Senior day. Stay cool. K.I.T.'

JULIUS. You didn't leave your number.

PRISCILLA. I remember, Julius.

JULIUS. I don't think you meant the part about staying cool, either.

PRISCILLA. I remember the senior prank.

JULIUS. So I forgive you, okay? You and your friends tied me naked to the flag pole. I would have laughed. Had things been totally different.

PRISCILLA. You know me.

JULIUS. Yes. Okay? Now that you mention it, yes. I remember you. What does that have to do with it? So, we went to the same high school. We're both mighty Cougars.

PRISCILLA. When did you know it was me?

JULIUS. Yes. Priscilla Strickland. Totally should have recognized you.

PRISCILLA. At what point, Julius? Or do you still go by Seagull?

JULIUS. Seagull, Julius. I don't know, okay?

PRISCILLA. What did I say in the poker room?

JULIUS. You said...

PRISCILLA. You knew before I came out here?!

JULIUS. You said... Yes. I knew. Priscilla Strickland.

PRISCILLA. And you were going to tell me...?

JULIUS. Soon. I promise. I kind of thought maybe you'd recognize me.

PRISCILLA. I don't remember saying anything about high school... why would I talk about that?

JULIUS. I told you what I do, right?

PRISCILLA. I can't believe you! Earlier this weekend, telling me I wasn't being up front, telling you about my scar. Who's hiding things?

JULIUS. I got you flowers. Where did I... Flowers! See?

PRISCILLA. From 7-11?

JULIUS. Well, they're open, aren't they?

PRISCILLA. Tell me the truth, Julius. I don't want flowers.

JULIUS. I got them. They had eleven. Okay? I wanted twelve, but they only had eleven. It's not a dozen, but what's perfect, right?

PRISCILLA. The flowers aren't the issue.

JULIUS. And... A castle! Look! I saw it and I thought of you!

PRISCILLA. A giant brick building? Am I supposed to swoon?!

JULIUS. Jesus. No, I thought. You said... You said you had defenses that you couldn't let down and here's this castle with a moat and giant stone walls and I thought of you, okay? There it is? Okay? I told you what I do, right?

PRISCILLA. Networks, right. IT.

JULIUS. Sure, yeah. Not exactly. Network consultant. Like people hire us if they want to know how secure their network is. Wasn't always like this, you know... I'm a hacker, that's what, I'm saying. And the poker room, well...

PRISCILLA. What? Jesus.

JULIUS. I found you. Totally random string search... Okay

ASYMMETRY

totally deliberate string search. Priscilla Strickland, login id '4-flushing'. Poker room password: 'gabby'. That's your... bird.

PRISCILLA. *(Simultaneously as 'That's')* My bird?

JULIUS. Right. So I joined the room. When you logged on.

PRISCILLA. Oh my god.

JULIUS. And I just happened to like the things you like at first and then... you know.

PRISCILLA. ...why? Why would you do that?

JULIUS. You know. For the-

PRISCILLA. *(Overlapping.)* Jesus. That was...

JULIUS. -K.I.T., right?

PRISCILLA. *(Gathering her things.)* No.

JULIUS. *(Going to her.)* No, no, that was a joke. I'm sorry.

PRISCILLA. What else do you know about me?

JULIUS. You know. Credit cards. E-mail passwords. Paypal info.

PRISCILLA. Really? Oh my god!

JULIUS. No, no. God, no, I'm kidding. Priscilla. You really should keep a better eye on that stuff, though. Crazies, you know.

(JULIUS stands in front of the door, blocking PRISCILLA's EXIT. PRISCILLA reaches into her purse and pulls out a can of mace.)

JULIUS. Whoah. *(Priscilla chases him away from door, threatening him with the mace.)*

PRISCILLA. *(Tries to EXIT.)* Get away from me.

JULIUS. Wait, I haven't. Wait.

(JULIUS shuts the door as soon as she's opened it.)

PRISCILLA. I'll spray you!

(She chases him across the apartment, holding the keychain-sized mace close to his eyes.)

JULIUS. I didn't-
PRISCILLA. What did you have planned?
JULIUS. Hold on-
PRISCILLA. To leave me somewhere? Naked? Tied to the-
JULIUS. *(Overlapping.)* No. No! I wasn't going to...
PRISCILLA. *(Retreating.)* I'll spray you. If you follow me.
JULIUS. *(Pursuing.)* Priscilla, please! It's not like that! Okay?

PRISCILLA. Don't follow me!

JULIUS. It isn't like that! I cyber-stalked you, okay? I found you, but... I found you, but...

PRISCILLA. What?

JULIUS. It changed, okay? I liked you. You were nice, like I didn't remember from high school.

PRISCILLA. You don't think people change? You think people should spend all eternity paying for the sins of high school? I paid, Julius. You think now I don't understand what you're going through? Look at me! Why can't you look at me?

JULIUS. I don't want to... you know... get sprayed in the eyes!

PRISCILLA. You don't think I'm sorry for being a bitch to you. I am, okay? I'm sorry for being a bitch to anyone who was, I don't know...

JULIUS. I forgive you! Can you put the mace away, please?
PRISCILLA. Look at me!

JULIUS. What, that thing again? You totally blow that out

ASYMMETRY

of proportion.

PRISCILLA. Are you serious?

JULIUS. Yes. I don't care about your face, okay?

PRISCILLA. You're such a liar.

JULIUS. You're the one who's so messed up about it. You're the one who thinks everyone's always looking at you.

PRISCILLA. Because they are-

JULIUS. *(Defiant.)* No! Look! I'm looking at you! I'm looking at you now, see?

PRISCILLA. You don't understand, I was beautiful.

JULIUS. You are beautiful.

PRISCILLA. No. I'm not, Julius. You can say it a hundred times and it won't make it true. You made me feel safe. You made me fall for you. You gave me hope that I was more than this thing that he did to me. That I could love someone and they could love me back.

JULIUS. I could. Please.

PRISCILLA. You said 'there's no one in the world like you' You called me your poker angel and said 'you'd let me win and let me win forever if it meant you'd always know me'. I believed you.

JULIUS. I wasn't lying then.

PRISCILLA. And everything that seemed so beautiful at three a.m., a thousand miles apart, now... just feels like make believe.

JULIUS. I wasn't lying then.

PRISCILLA. I don't know anymore. Tell me the truth, okay?

JULIUS. Anything.

PRISCILLA. You've hated me, haven't you? Ever since high school... you've hated me?

(JULIUS can't think of a lie quickly enough.)

ASYMMETRY

PRISCILLA. I'm leaving. Goodbye.
JULIUS. Wait. Wait. Priscilla!
PRISCILLA. *(Offstage.)* Don't follow me!

(He follows her offstage.)

JULIUS. *(Offstage.)* Please! Priscilla?! Please!

*(MAGGIE comes out of the bathroom and crosses to the bar to
    put her pipe and bag of weed away.
A knock at the front door summons MAGGIE. CODY waits at
    the threshold.)*

MAGGIE. You're back.
CODY. I'm sorry.
MAGGIE. Don't apologize.
CODY. Can I come in?
MAGGIE. Where are my manners? Of course.
CODY. *(Entering the living room.)* Your place smells like
bud.
MAGGIE. You want?
CODY. No.
MAGGIE. You don't...
CODY. No, I just...
MAGGIE. Wait.

(She traces a minute hand around her imaginary watch.)

MAGGIE. Yep. I'm baked. What can I do for you Mr...
CODY. First, ummm... Well, I was talking to the bartender
at the Saloon down the street and he says... don't let a some-

thing as simple as total incompatibility and random violence get in the way of a meaningful relationship.

MAGGIE. You're getting love advice from Fishy Peters?

CODY. You know him?

MAGGIE. *(Insinuating they're more than friends.)* Know him?

CODY. I don't really want to know. Look, I couldn't leave it like that. And now that I've had a few drinks, I thought, I'd... you know... walk back up here and tell you.

MAGGIE. You want to sit?

CODY. Umm... actually I just wanted to...

MAGGIE. You want a drink?

CODY. I should go.

MAGGIE. C'mon.

CODY. I just thought... can I call you? Maybe we could have some kind of you know... normal date.

MAGGIE. *(Sings, to Love on the Rocks.)* Scotch on the Rocks. Pour me a drink, and I'll tell you lies...

CODY. All right. Not sure I'd be... you know that much use behind the wheel right now, anyway.

MAGGIE. I'm sorry I hit you.

CODY. No. Forget about it. I'll black that whole part out tomorrow.

MAGGIE. You can do that? Selectively?

CODY. Not so much.

MAGGIE. *(Handing him a glass.)* Your drink. *(Pause.)* I haven't left you scarred, have I?

CODY. Uhh...

MAGGIE. I'd never forgive myself.

CODY. *(Pointing to his various wounds.)* Bite mark. Bite mark. Some scratches. You know, up and down here. Totally fine. Hurt so good.

ASYMMETRY

MAGGIE. Hand print.

CODY. You can see that?

MAGGIE. Oh, wait. Shit. Will you dance with me?

CODY. I'm not really... so much the good at dancing.

MAGGIE. I'll thrown you out. Really, I will. Out on the street.

CODY. I'm telling you, I've got nothing.

(MAGGIE picks a Billy Holiday song on her MP3 player.)

CODY. Ah. I love old... Who is this?

MAGGIE. Billie Holiday. Frame up. C'mon. I won't bite.

(CODY puts one arm behind her back and the other up and out. They rock back and forth in a slow circle more than actually dance. JULIUS enters through the front door and sulks back to the bedroom, defeated.)

MAGGIE. I almost blew it.

CODY. No.

MAGGIE. I did. I almost blew it.

CODY. I'm not really sure what to expect with you.

MAGGIE. I'm like a fucking... what was that...? Rubik's cube!

CODY. Yes!

MAGGIE. You're like... *(Miming someone trying to solve a Rubik's cube.)* Uh let's see here...

CODY. Right.

MAGGIE. I'm sorry. No, really.

CODY. No, it's fine.

MAGGIE. Just don't talk about love again, okay? Until I let you.

ASYMMETRY

CODY. Fine. Okay. You'll let me know?
MAGGIE. Absolutely.
CODY. I'm going to dip you now. Ready?
MAGGIE. Whoah! Aaaaah!

(He tries to finish the dance the song with a flourish, but he loses his balance and they both fall to the ground. He kisses her and she reciprocates. There's a moment of connection before MAGGIE snaps them out of it.)

MAGGIE. You want some more Scotch?
CODY. No, I'm fine.
MAGGIE. *(Jumping up to pour herself another.)* Don't mind if I do. *(Pause.)* What were you like when you were younger?
CODY. You wouldn't have liked me.
MAGGIE. Come on.
CODY. Seriously.
MAGGIE. You had bad hair?
CODY. How'd you know?
MAGGIE. Intuition.
CODY. I was idealistic. You know.
MAGGIE. M-hmm.
CODY. Do you know I got it on my first time?
MAGGIE. It...?
CODY. You know. Herpes.
MAGGIE. Really? I thought you got it in college.
CODY. Feeling lame now.
MAGGIE. Really?
CODY. Felt like Nietzsche. You know, one time and then...
MAGGIE. You obsess on this, you know.
CODY. You don't? You're on that herpessupport.com like four nights a week.

ASYMMETRY

MAGGIE. I'm just scamming guys you know. Like oh my god, it's so bad and they'll all...

CODY. You're joking?

MAGGIE. Of course. It's just so much more complex dating a clean guy, you know. With a clean guy there's just so many questions after sex. You know?

CODY. After?

MAGGIE. Yeah. Guys will ignore pretty much anything during.

CODY. Right. You are joking, right?

MAGGIE. Sure, yeah.

CODY. Right.

MAGGIE. What, you never gave it to anyone?

CODY. No. Are you serious?

MAGGIE. Really? Oh, yeah, sorry, I forgot.

CODY. I, you know remember it happening to me.

MAGGIE. I don't want to talk about it anymore.

CODY. Wait.

MAGGIE. Cody, c'mon. You're ruining it.

CODY. What am I ruining?

MAGGIE. The moment. C'mon, we were doing so well. Don't ruin it. C'mere.

CODY. No, wait a minute.

MAGGIE. C'mon, Cody.

CODY. What?

MAGGIE. Tell me you need me again. Tell me I'm your 'last shot'.

CODY. No, that's...

MAGGIE. I'll let you. Whisper to me.

(Pause.)

CODY. *(Definitive.)* No.
MAGGIE. Fine.
CODY. I can't, okay, maybe you were right...
MAGGIE. Fine.
CODY. Uhhh...
MAGGIE. What did you come back here for?
CODY. To apologize. For...
MAGGIE. For...
CODY. I'm actually not really sure. I have to go.
MAGGIE. Cody...
CODY. I'll call you.
MAGGIE. Fuck you, you'll call me.
CODY. I'm sorry.

(CODY EXITS and MAGGIE is left holding the Scotch, stunned. She stands there for a few moments, waiting for a knock at the door. She is joined by JULIUS who stands at the bar fidgeting with the glasses. MIGUEL enters and crosses to the picture of SANDY, JULIUS and PRISCILLA. This time, his curiosity gets the better of him and he circles the picture and looks down at it. He finally kneels over and picks the picture up. He covers his mouth with his hand. Something about it bothers him but he can't put his finger on it. There's a knock at the door, and, for a moment, it isn't clear who it is. A second knock. MAGGIE tries to shake off her disgust and EXITS to the bathroom. MIGUEL disappears into the bedroom, closing the door softly behind. JULIUS gathers his nerve and opens the door PRISCILLA is waiting, holding a scribbled on cocktail napkin, looking resolute.)

PRISCILLA. Hi.

ASYMMETRY

JULIUS. Hi. You left your stuff.

PRISCILLA. *(Marching into the living room.)* I was just going to leave it.

JULIUS. Sure. Sure. You know, I can sell most of that stuff black market. You know panties, bras...

PRISCILLA. Julius...

JULIUS. Sorry. Yes. I mean, hi. Can I... uhhh... get you like...

PRISCILLA. Listen? Can you listen? Please.

JULIUS. Yes. Absolutely. Totally.

PRISCILLA. I'm going to ask some questions, okay? Hold on, I wrote them down?

JULIUS. Wow. Are they hard? Sorry. Okay.

PRISCILLA. *(Reading.)* Did you spy on me in the poker room to get back at me?

JULIUS. Yes.

PRISCILLA. *(Reading.)* That one time, when we were playing with JackDaddy and OneEyedSix, where you got a straight, straight, flush-

JULIUS. I hacked it.

PRISCILLA. *(Reading.)* Did you use my bank account number or any of my passwords to read my e-mail or anything?

JULIUS. I uhh... Yes. I read your e-mail.

PRISCILLA. Okay. This one's not written down. How often?

JULIUS. You know early. I needed to know what you liked, you know. You know webmail is easily compromised by-

PRISCILLA. Okay. *(Reading.)* Did you see me naked today? In the shower?

JULIUS. No. I didn't. I totally didn't. Your feet, that's it. And knees. A tiny part of the thigh. But none of your... parts. Okay?

ASYMMETRY

PRISCILLA. And. Lastly... did you mean that castle thing to be nice?

JULIUS. Yes. Totally. Can I give it to you now? Is that okay?

PRISCILLA. Okay.

(JULIUS practically lunges for the gift on the table and collects himself smoothly before handing it to her. He mimes a miniature version of himself scaling the walls to get through her defensives.)

JULIUS. I thought, you know this is you and I could be like... here I come over the walls... you know. It's awkward, I know. I have no poetry. I have no gift for self-expression.

PRISCILLA. I think you do.

JULIUS. But... and this is continuing in my policy of being totally honest. Okay? *(Pause.)* I love you. I love you. I'm sorry.

PRISCILLA. It's okay. You can cry.

JULIUS. It's just. You left. And...

PRISCILLA. I'm back. You've got to let a girl... you know adjust to new circumstances.

JULIUS. I'm not really Seagull anymore.

PRISCILLA. That's fine. I like-

JULIUS. Work frowns on it, you know.

PRISCILLA. I like Julius anyway.

JULIUS. Priscilla, can I touch you? I mean, can I...

PRISCILLA. Okay. Carefully...

(JULIUS breaches the loose spatial relationship and she meets his hand halfway and places it on her scarred cheek. Black-out.)

End of play

ASYMMETRY

PROP LIST

Safari-themed luggage
Handbag
Towel
Wallet containing a little cash
Keys
Bottle of Scotch
2 Highball glasses
Prescription bottle filled with pills
Poetry journal
Blanket
Miniature plastic castle
11 Individually wrapped roses
Bag of 'weed'
Small pipe
Photograph
Yearbook
Small can of mace
MP3 player/speaker combo or CD player
Cocktail napkin

COSTUME/MAKE-UP GUIDELINES

The period is modern, contemporary and the play takes place over the course of one single evening. There are no quick changes. Most costume changes take place in real time as characters change clothes/disrobe during their scenes.

There is a make up effect needed. Priscilla's scar takes up most of the right side of her face, causing her eyelid to droop slightly. Scar effect make-up and prosthetic is required.

Other Important Notes: All characters end up revealing themselves physically as well as emotionally throughout the play. The characters in this production ended up in the color exact same shade of red at their most vulnerable and used other colors to cover up physically as in Maggie, Cody, Miguel and Sandy's case or metaphorically as Priscilla and Julius were concerned.

ASYMMETRY

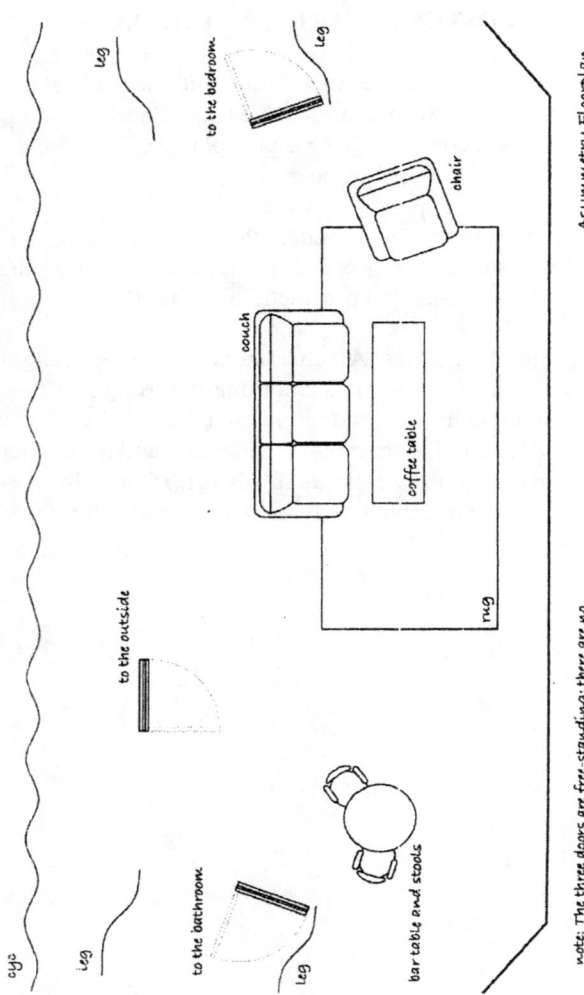

Asymmetry Floorplan

note: The three doors are free-standing; there are no walls to bound the action, and the cyc should be lit to reflect the mood of the play as it progresses.

OTHER TITLES AVAILABLE FROM SAMUEL FRENCH

THE DEW POINT

Neena Beber

2m, 3f

Can a woman be friends with a womanizer – even if she once dated him herself? And if your best friend wants to date the guy, do you stand in her way? *The Dew Point* is a play about love and marriage, sex and friendship, authenticity and blackmail...and the lies we tell in order to stay honest.

"...A comedy of sexual manners whose characters are funny yet sympathetic and complexly believable...The success of this deceptively labeled "romantic comedy" lies in the way it zeroes in on the way we deceive others by deceiving ourselves, plumping the bread of friendship into some pretty rancid sandwiches that are, of course, proffered with the best of intentions."
– Carolyn Clay, *Boston Phoenix*

"It is a pleasure to report that *The Dew Point* by Neena Beber, who won a *Village Voice* OBIE last season for emerging playwright, is an intelligent, well constructed, contemporary drama with sharp, bright, witty dialogue and fully detailed vibrant, believeable characters."
– Bob Rendell, *Talkin' Broadway*

HALF AND HALF

James Sherman

Comedy / 1m, 2f / Unit Set

In *Half and Half,* James Sherman explores marriages past and present in two related one-act plays. In the first act, set at a breakfast in 1970, the breadwinner husband reads the newspaper and the homemaker wife fries the eggs. In act two, at a breakfast taking place this morning, the career-minded wife reads the paper and the stay-at-home husband cooks the frittata. With his unique comic insight, Sherman looks at how husbands and wives accept and reject their roles, how their roles have changed and, how their roles just might be changing back.

The same three actors portray the age appropriate roles in each act, creating an interesting parallel between the two generations, making for a very poignant comedy about marriage.

OTHER TITLES AVAILABLE FROM SAMUEL FRENCH

IDENTICAL SAME TEMPTATION

Bob Glaudini

2m, 2f / Comedy / Interior

A new contemporary comedy of sex and manners that looks at two girlfriends who try to create their ideal mate through the personalities of twin brothers, with outrageous results.